CHRISTM

by

Arie Van der Ende

Text copyright 2018 by Arie Van der Ende. All rights reserved. No part of this work

may be reproduced or transmitted in any form or by any means, without the written permission of the copyright holder.

INDEX

Screwheart

Can Eberling Screwheart, a crotchety old tightwad, be touched by the Christmas spirit because of a sweet little girl's naïveté?

Jenny and Emily

Can a mother's neglect and a husband's abuse lead to a happy Christmas holiday celebration?

The miracle

The year is 1944. War is raging in Europe. Resistance against occupation is strong. A young couple is caught in the turmoil. Hunger and cruelty is everywhere. Is a miracle possible in the midst of all this?

SCREWHEART

by

Arie Van der Ende

"God bless us, everyone."

Charles Dickens (The Christmas Carol) – 1812 - 1870

Eberling Screwheart was a crotchety old man of few words, who, when he did speak, often spewed sarcasm and vitriol. He frequently punctuated his pronouncements with his favorite word, "Blast!".

He grumbled about 'blasted weather' when it was raining, 'blasted contraption' when his umbrella wouldn't unfold properly or 'blasted government' when anything adversely affected his money or his comfort.

Now in his mid-eighties, Screwheart walked with a slight stoop. His hair had receded and his nose and ears stuck out like protuberances on a tree. His eyes, though watery at times, were still an intense blue and flickered with tenacity, as they peered out from under snowy white bushy eyebrows.

Back when the aftermath of World War II presented the opportunity, he had invested every penny he could in real estate near large cities and reaped a small fortune as a result.

Screwheart may have been a shrewd investor, but he wasn't so good at being a pleasant person. Kindness, charity and generosity were anathema to him and he rebuffed every attempt to separate him from even a tiny portion of his accumulated wealth.

    He had lived his whole life that way, always striving for material things but shunning feelings of tenderness and love. He looked upon other people as potential threats to his possessions and remained a bachelor. He never knew the thrill of having someone to love, the caress of a warm hearted woman or the joys of fatherhood and the adoration of children.

    He guarded his belongings with a passion and lived a life of frugality that would do a miser proud.

He made his home in a cheap walk-up apartment in a run down neighbourhood he was eyeing for a possible future purchase. His furnishings were sparse and worn and his pantry was bare, save for a few cans of food discarded by a grocer as being well beyond their expiry date.

He ate only twice a day and his diet consisted mainly of gruel in the morning and a scrap of meat and some day-old bread at night. He kept the temperature in his rooms at 58 degrees and wore his patched sweaters day and night.

Friends or companions he had none. He received his daily news from a small black and white television set, hooked up to a wire coat hanger for an antenna. His water heater was broken and his cold water faucet produced a sputtering stream of rust coloured water.

He drove an ancient Chevy and kept it going by fixing only what was absolutely necessary to keep it running. He patched up anything else with duct tape and with whatever he could scrounge from the wrecking yard or the dump. The exhaust pipes had several folded over tin cans holding them together and the doors could be shut only part way. The engine coughed and complained when an attempt was made to wake it from its lethargy. The battery was old and often refused to cooperate. When that happened, he was not averse to accepting a boost from a stranger. Being loath to give help to others, did not prevent him from accepting it for himself.

It was the start of December in Southwestern Ontario. The days were frigid and the nights were cold. Most of the birds had fled South long ago. A thin layer of snow was covering the fields. There had been a few snowstorms already, but they had been followed by short periods of thaw.

The leaves of the trees had fallen long ago and their branches were sticking up naked to the sky like the outstretched arms of skeletons in a black and white cartoon. The whole world was in mourning, it seemed, and waiting for the harsh winter to come. A few screeching blue jays were scrounging for scraps of discarded food near garbage cans. Other winter birds, such as cardinals and chickadees, kept to the woods. The roads were slushy and dirty with the remnants of snowbanks.

Screwheart rummaged through his old refrigerator for his evening meal but found only a torn package of luncheon meat, long past its "best before" date. He picked it up and sniffed it. It smelled like an unwashed armpit and its colour had turned an ominous green, It sprouted a few hairs and looked like an experimental test sample in a laboratory. He threw it back in disgust and looked around for his wallet.

He pulled out a five dollar bill and grunted, "I wonder if Joe's diner might give me something to eat for this. It's late in the day and he must have some left over food from his supper customers."

He put on his winter coat and jammed his trusty "trapper's hat", with the furry ear flaps, on his head. He pulled his collar tight around his neck and stumbled down the stairs. He found his snow covered car waiting for him in the alley and turned the key. Amazingly, the car started after only a half dozen cranks and blew a cloud of black smoke and a fart from its exhaust pipe. He brushed the snow off the windshield and set off. The heater had given up long ago and he shivered in his worn coat.

Joe's diner was located about two miles out of town and had been there for as long as anyone could remember. It had been started by Joe's father when there had been talk of a highway being built near there. When that hadn't materialized, the diner was surviving by providing cheap meals and watered down booze to the locals.

Screwheart drove toward his destination. The old car sputtered and popped but somehow hung together. Its balding tires couldn't get a solid grip on the slippery road surface and often drifted into a partial spin. It was all Screwheart could do to keep it on the road.

As he left the town behind and entered the open road, the wind started to pick up and snow drifted at an angle towards him. He put the windshield wipers on. Only one of them worked, but, fortunately, it was the one on the driver's side.

When he came to a curve just past an old farm house, a patch of ice on the road was the last punishment his tires could endure. They gave up their doomed struggle and the car slid sideways into the ditch. It rolled over, crashed through a barbed wire fence and came to rest, right side up, at the edge of a field. Screwheart tumbled out through the door and got his left leg stuck under the vehicle – its engine still running. Struggle as he might, he couldn't pull it out from under the wreck.

"Now what in blazes am I going to do?" he muttered. He was lying on his back and stared at the rapidly darkening sky. Hesitantly, the first stars were becoming visible and a wan moon was rising at the horizon.

His warm winter hat had stayed strapped to his head and his coat still covered him, but the frigid air chilled him to the bone. He realized that he could not stay long in this position without serious consequences.

The engine sputtered and then died. The headlights began to dim and blinked out. He was all alone, in the dark and losing body heat fast.

A few cars whizzed by on the road, but, even though he yelled at the top of his voice, not one of them stopped. He doubted that anyone could hear him. Or even see him in the dark, him being well off the road.

He started to worry. What would happen to him if nobody came to rescue him? "I'll probably freeze to death and no-one would even care," he mumbled, "I have no blasted friends to mourn me, no relatives to even remember me."

The "Aurora Borealis", the Northern Lights, started to dance across the sky. Flames of brilliant emerald green and cobalt blue swept up and down the sky, shimmering from horizon to horizon in a constantly changing pattern. A magic water colour brush then added streaks of magenta to the vivid and surrealistic masterpiece being painted in the heavens. A shooting star, seemingly originating from the pale moon, completed the illusion that the founder of impressionism, Claude Monet, had awakened from his eternal slumbers and put on a display for all the world to see.

Screwheart couldn't help but admire the view above him, but he also couldn't help feeling very much afraid that he was doomed to die in a lonely field, pinned under his car and all alone. His leg had gone numb. He had stopped shivering and started to lose the feeling in his extremities. He knew that he was in deep trouble.

Then, glory be!. He heard someone walking on the road, boots scraping on the gravel at the edge of the pavement. He could hardly believe his ears. He twisted his head to see. A dark shape was slowly moving toward him, backlit by the pale moonlight. It moved steadily in his direction,

Screwheart breathed in deeply and then let out a roar like a wounded animal, "Help, please, help. I'm down here!"

The figure stopped, apparently unsure about the sound, so he yelled again. "Help, please help. Help!"

To his relief, he received an answer. It was a woman's voice. "Hello! Is anyone down there?"

"Yes," he yelled, "I'm down here. There's been an accident. Who are you? Are you a blasted woman? Come and help me!"

The woman scrambled through the ditch, skirted the ruined fence posts and tangled barbed wire and came toward him. She said, "What have you got against women? Especially the ones you're asking for help?"

Screwheart craned his neck to get a better look at his would-be rescuer. The feeble moonlight illuminated a slender middle aged woman, with a kind face and bundled up in a heavy duffel coat more suited to a man. He said,

"Women are weak and cry a lot. But never mind that, help me get out from under this blasted car!"

The woman made no attempt to comply, but said, "Women are stronger than you think. What happened here?"

Screwheart gritted his teeth and angrily shook his head. "That's a stupid question! Have you never seen a blasted car wreck before? Get this stupid car off me, woman!"

"How do you expect me to do that? And don't call me woman. My name is Christine. Christine Undermere. I'll go home and call 911 for you. They'll send a tow truck and an ambulance. By the way, what's your name?"

Screwheart didn't reply, but said, "I don't need a blasted ambulance. Or a tow truck either. I'll get somebody to pull my car out without paying some blasted towing company. Just get this car off my leg."

"I can't lift a car. It's way too heavy."

"I thought you said you were strong?"

"Not strong enough to lift a car. A man couldn't do it either."

"Well then, get yourself a blasted lever! My God, women are so helpless."

It was a wonder that she took his verbal abuse without leaving him there, but she didn't. The seriousness of the situation was apparent and she felt an obligation to help. She said, "Look, you're in trouble. I'll call 911 whether you like it or not. This is no time for . . . "

Screwheart didn't give her a chance to finish. He interrupted, "I don't want a blasted ambulance. If you don't want to help me, then leave and let me die."

Christine looked at him with pity. "You are a bitter old man, aren't you? I'm just trying to help. If there were a way to free you, I'd do it, but . . . "

Screwheart fumbled for her in the dark, grabbed her by the hand and said, "But there is, . . . uh . . . Christine. My name is Eberling Screwheart and I do appreciate your help. Get one of those blas . . . I mean . . . one of those fence posts, stick it under the edge of the car and pull up. You'll need to lift it only a few inches so I can pull my leg out. Please do it. And I promise to get a blasted doctor to look at my leg after I get free."

Christine, apparently immune to his abuse, and with an innate desire to help, said, "But there's a lot of barbed wire attached to those posts. It's going to be difficult to get one close enough to the car."

"There's one sticking in my back. Use that one."

Christine complied. "I hope I'll be strong enough," she muttered.

Screwheart heard her and said, "Come on, woman, you're only half my age. You can do it."

"I told you. Call me Christine," she said as she shoved the pole under the car and pulled up on it. But the ground had not yet frozen solid and the end of the pole merely sank into the soft earth.

"You need a fulcrum," Screwheart said, "Use that rock over there," pointing to a large stone. "You do know what a fulcrum is, don't you?"

"Yes, I know what a fulcrum is," Christine said, with a sigh.

She got the stone, placed it close to the car and said, "O.K., now put your good leg against the car. When I push down on the lever, push hard against the car and yank your stuck leg out quickly. I won't be able to hold the car up for very long."

"I know, I know. Get on with it!" he growled.

Christine pushed down on the slippery fence post as hard as she could and managed to raise the car a scant few inches. Screwheart did just as Christine had directed him and got himself free.

As the car crashed back to its original position Christine let go of the pole. It jerked sideways and hit Screwheart in the back.

"Blast it all, you hit me! Why can't you be more careful!"

"I'm sorry, it slipped out of my hands. That thing was covered with frozen snow, you know."

"Well, watch it from now on."

Christine was finally getting fed up with Screwheart's rants. She said, "I don't intend to ever do this again. I should have called 911 in the first place. This was all your crazy idea." She relented immediately. "Are you hurt anywhere?" she asked.

"No, I don't think so. Just help me get back on the road."

"You're not going anywhere. I'll take you to my house, just over there, to get you cleaned up. Then I'll take you to the hospital for a check-up. I'll ask my neighbour to drive us."

Screwheart didn't answer but reached for her shoulder to lean on as they scrambled through the ditch and to the road.

"My house is just there about 150 yards away," Christine said, pointing to a large two story brick farm house.

With Screwheart leaning on the woman for support, they slowly walked toward the house in the dark. It was almost ten o'clock and all traffic had ceased on the road.

"Is your husband there waiting for us?" Screwheart asked.

Christine slowed down and said, with a lump in her throat, "My husband died almost two years ago," She did not elaborate.

With the blood now flowing freely through his veins, Screwheart's leg seemed to improve as they walked. He said, "I'm almost as good as new now, so I don't want to go to the hospital. Probably all I got were a few scrapes. Nothing to worry about."

Christine, after a short pause, said, "We'll see after we get your leg cleaned up. I'll be able to tell better then. I'm a nurse, you know. "

As they approached the house, Screwheart asked, "What were you doing on the road at night? Going out for a blasted stroll?"

Christine didn't answer immediately, then said, "What's wrong with you? Do you have to blast everything you talk about?"

"You didn't answer my question. Do you usually walk alone on the road, in the dark?"

"What are you implying? I was coming back from my neighbour's place. She's a widow too and her milk cow was giving birth. I helped her deliver her newborn calf. Country folk help each other, you know. What were *you* doing? Out sightseeing?" she asked sarcastically.

'I'll have you know that I was going to Joe's diner for a meal."

They arrived and entered through the back door directly into a large country kitchen.

A heavy set woman helped them in and said, "Christine, you're late. Is everything alright? And who's this?" She looked suspiciously at Screwheart.

"This is Mr. Eberling Screwheart," Christine said, "He had an accident with his car and hurt his leg." To Screwheart, she said, "This is Margaret Clapstone, my neighbour and my friend."

Screwheart grunted something in acknowledgement.

Addressing her friend, Christine asked. "Marge, did you get my kids to bed alright?"

The woman helped her put Screwheart on a kitchen chair to clean him up and answered, "Oh yeah, Chris, no problem at all. They're little angels and prayed for you and even for the little calf to come."

Christine thanked Marge for looking after her little girls and sent her home with some home made cookies. "I'll call you tomorrow," she promised.

Screwheart's leg had some scrapes, and there was a small cut just below the knee, but it seemed alright otherwise.

"You were lucky to survive your accident so well, my friend," Christine said. "Do you have any family you want me to call for you?"

"No I have no blasted family. I live alone."

Christine took charge immediately. "Well then, you'd better stay here tonight. I have a lazy-boy chair in the parlour. My husband used to sleep in that chair on occasion. You can use it tonight. We'll see what to do with you in the morning. And, by the way, we must call the police and report the accident. When they see the wreck, they'll want to investigate."

Screwheart shook his head. "No police need to be involved. That old car isn't worth a tinker's damn. It's decades old and held together with wire and a curse. I'll call the junkyard to haul it out of there. I presume you have a phone?"

Christine cringed at his language, sighed and, pointing to a dial wall phone in the corner of the kitchen, said, "O.K. Have it your way. The phone is over there,"

Screwheart stumbled to the phone, lifted it and dialed the wrecking yard. He knew the number by heart because of his many dealings with them over the years when patching up his old Chevy.

"Hello. Is that you, Pete? Sorry to call you at home. But my old clunker has finally given up the ghost. It slid off the road tonight and I'll give it to you as a present. You can have it for parts. What? . . . No, if you'll come and get it, I wont ask you for any money. You can have it for free, just don't charge me for hauling it out. . . . Yeah, I know it isn't worth a tinker's damn," he said, repeating the phrase, "But there are still good parts in it . . . You'll have to come and get it first thing in the morning. . . . Yeah, at daybreak or before . . . Hang on."

He turned to Christine and asked, "What's your address here?"

Turning back to the phone, he said, "Pete, the address is 41239 Dodger's road, just past a large farmhouse. . . . O.K. It's a deal, but first thing, O.K.?" He hung up.

Christine looked at him sternly and said, "I offered to let you stay the night and I've even given you something to eat but don't you swear in my house, not even as a figure of speech! I don't want any profanity around my little girls. Understood? Even your "blasted" expression is not appreciated. So curb your tongue."

Screwheart didn't say anything, ate his sandwich in silence and settled in the parlour as offered.

- - - - - - - - -

Screwheart slept soundly that night. He had to get up to use the bathroom a few times but settled again in the chair without trouble. In fact, that lazy-boy was more comfortable than his own lumpy bed.

When he awoke, he had the feeling that someone was staring at him. The back of his neck felt itchy, He slowly opened his eyes. For a moment he didn't know where he was, but when he heard someone in the kitchen moving around, he remembered. But the eerie, tingly feeling remained.

He looked around the room and saw a young girl, clad in pyjamas, staring at him with the bluest eyes he'd ever seen. She was less than four feet tall and just stood there. Her thick curly blond hair cascaded to her waist. She looked like a little angel on a religious tract. She had a serious expression on her face.

He pulled the footrest of his chair shut and sat up straight. He said, "Who are you?" and pulled the blanket close around himself.

The little girl said, "My name is Mary. I'm six, almost seven. Who are you?"

Screwheart had always thought of children as a nuisance and a hindrance and he was intrigued. He said, "You shouldn't come into a man's bedroom."

Mary said, "Silly! This isn't a bedroom. It's the parlour. Why don't you want to give me your name? Everybody has a name. What's yours?"

"O.K. if you must know, My name is Mr. Screwheart."

The girl frowned and said, "Screw . . . ha . . . That's too long. I'll just call you Mr. Screw. Yah, that's better." She savoured the sound. "Screw . . . yah, that's it. Mommy said you hurt your leg. Sometimes I hurt *my* leg when I fall on the gravel stones." She switched to a new subject immediately and said, "How come you have no hair on your head? I have hair on my head. Mommy does too. Where is yours?"

Screwheart had rarely talked to little girls and was fascinated by her chatter. He said, "When you get old, your follicles shrink and then disappear."

"What's folli . . . whatever you said?" Not waiting for an answer, she rambled on, "Mommy is old and her foll . . follies didn't disappear."

She came over and ran her hand over his bald pate. "Feels nice and smooth, Just like an apple." Taking his face in her tiny hands, she lifted it up. "Oh, I know where it went. It's sprouting on your face." She rubbed his cheeks. "Yah, I can feel it coming out."

Screwheart pulled away from her. "I haven't had time to shave yet. Haven't you ever seen a man before?"

"Oh yes," the girl assured him. "My Daddy is a man. But he's gone to Heaven now. He can't come home. We have to go see him there some day. Mommy told me."

The girl's naïveté amused Screwheart and he was about to say something, when a voice from the kitchen called, "Mary, where are you? Breakfast is ready."

Mary answered with her little girl's squeaky voice. "I'm here, Mommy, with Mr. Screw. We're talking."

Christine came to the parlour door and said, "Come on, Mary, don't bother Mr. Screwheart."

Coming to the girl's defence, Screwheart said, "Oh, she's not bothering me. She's a delightful little girl."

"Well, come on, Mary. And you, Mr. Screwheart, will you have some breakfast with us? It's all ready."

"Give me a minute to get dressed and I'll be there."

Mary went with her mother and a few minutes later, Screwheart joined them at the large kitchen table. The aroma of bacon, sausages and pancakes filled the room.

"Would you like to say grace for us, Mr. Screwheart?" Christine asked.

"Well, , , uh . . . no. I don't . . . uh . . . "

Mary piped up. "I'll help you, Mr. Screw. Just say 'Dear father . . . " she stopped and said, "I told you my Daddy is in Heaven. There's another Daddy there, but he's called a Father."

Christine interrupted, "It's O.K. Mary. Leave Mr. Screwheart alone. *You* can say the grace this morning."

Mary, obediently folded her hands, and, peeking through half-shut eye lids at Screwheart, said, "Dear Father in Heaven, bless this food for us and take care of my Daddy. Tell him I say hi. And also, bring my little sister Cathy a new heart, so she can breathe better. Oh, and show Mr. Screw how to talk to you. He hurt his leg, so he has trouble walking. Maybe he needs a new one too. I guess that's all for now. I'll talk to you later . . . Amen."

Turning to Screwheart, she said, "That's how you say goodbye to people in Heaven."

Christine said, "Sorry, Mr. Screwheart, she likes to talk a blue streak."

"It's O.K." he replied, "but what's this about little Cathy? Is she your other daughter?"

"Yes she is. When she was born, her heart wasn't working quite right and we've been doctoring with her ever since. A community nurse comes in every day to take care of her, and gives her medication. But Cathy needs a heart transplant. At her age – she's not even three years old – it's hard to find a suitable donor. We've been waiting for over two years already and she's slowly getting worse. At this rate, she'll . . ." She swallowed and a painful look crossed her face.

She continued, "And, anyways, I feel terrible about a transplant. Not only is that a serious operation on a little child like Cathy, but I shudder to think that another little girl or boy would need to die before . . . " She choked back a tear.

Mary shoved her chair back and ran to her. "Mommy, don't cry. That other little girl is going to be with Daddy. She can keep him company until I get there."

Christine hugged her tight and kissed her tenderly.

Screwheart started to feel very uncomfortable. He was not used to having so much love around him. All his life he had been surrounded by greedy and egotistical people who were out for one thing only: How to get rich. And if that was caused by someone's misery and suffering, so be it.

No-one talked for a while. . .

Then Mary, still chewing the last of her sausage, asked, "Mommy, can I go and read to Cathy?"

Christine, like thousands of mothers before her, admonished the little girl, "May I, Mary, may I."

Mary, dutifully repeated, "May I Mommy?"

Receiving her mother's permission, Mary sprang up from her chair and bolted from the room.

Screwheart watched her go and said, "Little kids don't ever walk, do they? They only know how to run."

Christine agreed. "They're full of energy." Switching subjects, she asked, "What are your plans now, Mr. Screwheart?"

"Well, I hadn't really . . . " Screwheart hesitated. "I . . .

"

"Look, I have a proposition. You said you live alone and have no family. In a few weeks, it'll be Christmas. Why don't you stay with us until after the holidays? You seem to like it here and Mary could do with some male companionship. And she has taken to you. What do you say?"

"I am flattered that you would . . . Oh, Christine, do you really mean it? Yes, I would very much like that. But won't I be in the way? Would you want an old codger hanging around and bothering you?"

"You won't bother me, provided you behave yourself. If you don't, out you go. If that is clearly understood, I'll be . . . *we'll* be happy to have you. You can make yourself useful by babysitting my kids once in a while and fix some small repairs that may be needed."

He started to correct her, "You don't "fix" repairs, you . . . ", but he quickly swallowed his criticism and said, instead, "I'd be most happy to. I'm pretty good at it, too."

Christine watched him stumble over his words and took it as a sign that he was trying, "That's a good thing," she thought.

She continued, "You can teach Mary about things. But I absolutely expect no hanky-panky, no swearwords, no crazy ideas. She's very impressionable and picks up on things fast. You're going to have to be a kind and loving grandpa to her."

She was quiet for a few seconds and then said, "My father died when he was only in his early sixties and the Lord took my husband to his glory just when I needed him most. Mary misses her father terribly too and constantly talks about him.

"One other thing, Mr. Screwheart. This is a Christian home and all its occupants are expected to abide by its principles. If you can't do that, say so now and the deal is off."

Screwheart looked at her and said, "You really believe in God, don't you?"

Christine replied, "It's quite obvious to me that there is a supreme power in this vast universe, who originated everything and keeps it all together. We call that power 'God' and it behooves us to acknowledge Him. Mary has a simplistic view of these things and that is refreshing. It teaches us that a child-like belief is more to be desired than a sophisticated agnostic doubt.

"It is equally obvious that there are lots of bad things happening in the world. Generally, we have made a mess of all the wonderful opportunities and gifts that are available to us. Later this month, we'll be celebrating the birth of our Saviour, who came to forgive us for that and show us the way to behave properly.

"If you believe that's what the Christmas baby represents, you'll have to admit that it was the greatest possible thing that happened in the history of the universe, and therefore the most important event to be celebrated. Would you like to celebrate it with us, Mr. Screwheart?"

Deeply touched, Screwheart walked over to her, took her hands in his and said, "Dear Christine, I have not yet thanked you for saving my life. I do so now and promise you that I will never forget what you have done for me. And your kind offer is much appreciated. I will most gratefully accept it and thank you for trusting me with your precious children. I swear on my word of honour that I will try to do my very best to deserve that trust and will never disappoint you.

"As regards your belief in God, if you and your little daughter are an example of Christian living, I want that too and am anxious to learn from you how to do that.

"One thing, though. Please call me Eberling, not Mr. Screwheart. If we're going to be close friends, that seems appropriate."

Solemnly, they shook hands.

- - - - - - - - -

Mary loved her Mr. Screw and the two bonded as grandpa and his little grandchild. They often turned off the television set after supper so Screwheart could regale Mary with tales of Sherlock Holmes mysteries, Harry Potter fantasies, and the geographical exploits of Dr. David Livingstone in Africa. When doing so, he would vary the pitch, the tone and the timbre of his voice to emulate the various characters in the story.

Even Christine was fascinated by his performance and she was never sorry she had invited him to share her home with him. She started to look upon him as her substitute father and they all lived happily together in the old farmhouse.

A constant shadow hanging over them, however, was the slowly deteriorating health of little Cathy. She was getting the best of care, but medical science was limited in what could be done for her.

Over the past two years it had became clear that the only solution was a heart replacement. But time and again they had been disappointed. When, on rare occasions, a donor heart became available, it hadn't been a suitable match for Cathy and she had to wait yet again. Every day they prayed and waited.

But then, about two weeks after Screwheart's arrival, when Christine had gone grocery shopping with Margaret Clapstone, her neighbour, and Screwheart was babysitting the little girls, there was a telephone call. Screwheart answered it. A nurse from the University Hospital in London, Ontario, was on the line.

After Screwheart identified himself as a friend of the family and told the nurse that Christine was not then available, the nurse asked him to reach her as soon as possible.

She said, "There's news about Cathy's transplant. The little girl must get here as soon as possible. We think we have a good match and she must come in for the preliminary tests and procedures. If everything works out, the operation may take place later today. The donated heart is coming in from California and should be transplanted as soon as it arrives, while it is still fresh. I've already called your local ambulance service to pick her up. It should be there shortly."

Screwheart assured her that he would do all he could to get Christine to the hospital and hung up. He called the police station to explain the situation and was given a promise that they would round up Christine forthwith.

Then he sat down with Mary, who had watched the flurry of activity with wide open eyes and a worried look on her face. He explained that, at last, her little sister was slated to be operated on that day and would be taken to the hospital as soon as the ambulance arrived. He said, "The University Hospital is one of the best in the country and is known worldwide for its excellent reputation in transplant procedures. Your little sister has the best chance of coming through this very serious operation done by the very best doctors."

Mary took all of that in without saying anything for a full five minutes, but then said, "We must ask the Father, the one in Heaven, to help Cathy. We must pray to him. Will you help me?"

Screwheart, overcome with emotion, almost burst into tears, but hugged his adopted grandchild and said, "Yes, sweetheart, let's do just that. You start and I'll join you."

Mary folded her hands and said, "Dear Father in Heaven. This is Mary. Cathy is going to get a new heart. Please make sure that it is nice and clean and help those doctors to fit it in just right. Tell Cathy I'm here, waiting to play with her. Now here's Mr. Screw. He wants to say something." She moved her folded hands toward Screwheart as though to hand him a telephone.

Screwheart took her little hands into his big calloused ones and, bowing his head, said, "Lord, I've not prayed since I was a little child, but I'm praying to you now. I'm begging you to help this family and make the operation successful. Not for my sake. I don't deserve anything, but these are good people and they deserve a break. I beg you . . . " He choked back his tears and couldn't go on.

Mary hugged him.

The ambulance screamed into the yard, the paramedics jumped out with a gurney between them and entered the house. They were familiar with the layout, having been there many times before.

In no time they had little Cathy strapped to the gurney just as Christine and her friend drove into the driveway, accompanied by a police cruiser.

Screwheart swiftly brought her up to date and she, grinning with joy, but with apprehension clouding her face, joined the paramedics in the ambulance. In mere seconds they left, sirens wailing.

Margaret said, "The police found us before we could pay for our groceries so we just ran out of the store and followed the police car. I have them here, but we still haven't paid for them."

Screwheart assured her that he would take care of it and not to worry. Margaret, a kindhearted lady, thanked him and made him promise to let her know as soon as he learned the outcome of the operation.

All afternoon, Screwheart paced up and down the kitchen floor, staying close by the phone for news from Christine.

He scrambled some eggs for his and Mary's supper. Mary was a bundle of nerves, anxiously hugging herself in a corner of the room. She asked him a dozen times to explain the operation to her and he did the best he could.

Finally, late in the evening, Christine telephoned. "Oh Eberling," she said, "The operation was a great success. Cathy is now resting comfortably. She's breathing so much better. I'm so happy! Are you and Mary making out alright? Did you have anything to eat tonight?"

When Screwheart assured her they were fine and rejoiced with her, Christine, still worried about her family, said, "I'm going to call Marge and ask her to stop by and cook you some dinner each day. There should be enough food in the 'fridge to do that.

"Cathy has to stay here for several more days and I'm going to stay with her. But, Eberling, I may be able to take her home for Christmas. Won't that be wonderful? I'll stay in touch and let you know."

- - - - - - - - -

As predicted by the doctors, Christine arrived home shortly after lunch on the day before Christmas. She walked in with her youngest child cradled in her arms.

Mary rushed to her and looked with awe at her little sister, sound asleep in her warm covering blanket. The constant struggle to breathe, that had plagued her for years, was now a thing of the past. Her little breast was rising and falling in the rhythmic pattern of peaceful, restful sleep.

Christine said, "It's so good to be home with the best, most wonderful Christmas present of all." She laid the child in her bed and gently closed the door.

Turning to Screwheart, she said, "Eberling, I've been thinking while in London these past few days. We now have a wonderful little family. I want you to stay with us. Not just as a guest, but for always. We have lots of room, we love you and we don't want you to leave. Please say you will."

Screwheart took her hands in his and, with tears in his eyes, said, "Dear Christine, now that I have experienced life within your loving family, I would like nothing better than to accept. It's the most generous and kind offer I have ever received in my whole life – an offer I will treasure for as long as I live.

"And. Christine, I will continue to love your delightful children as their own grandpa. I will set up a trust fund for their education and devote all my finances and energies to their welfare, and to yours, for the rest of my life."

Mary looked at her mother. "Mommy, does that mean Mr. Screw is gonna stay with us forever?" She clapped her hands. "Oh goody! Just like the story of Mr . . . uh . . . Mr. Dick . . . Dicky. You know . . . "The Christmas Carol". There was a little boy in that story. He said it the bestest. "God bless us, everyone!"

THE END

JENNY and EMILY

by

Arie Van der Ende

The greater the power, the more dangerous the abuse.

Edmund Burke 1729 - 1797

Five year old Jenny Jones was becoming anxious. All day she had been waiting for her mother to return. She'd had no lunch and was getting very hungry. She found a piece of cheese in the refrigerator and washed it down with some water from the kitchen sink.

Jenny clambered on the threadbare couch in the corner of the kitchen. Carefully avoiding a broken spring sticking through a torn cushion, she leaned back and dozed off.

The shabby apartment consisted of a fair sized kitchen with a small window overlooking a parking lot, a cramped two piece bathroom, and a small bedroom. There was no living room.

Jenny was an only child. Her mother, frequently high on drugs, often called her "my mistake". She wasn't referring to birthing the little girl, but conceiving her in the first place. That shouldn't have been a surprise however. To support her addiction, she spread her legs whenever it meant getting some ready cash.

Her name was Lucille, but at the tavern, where she worked, she was known as Louizy. The people there called her "Easy – Louizy" behind her back. Not only did that refer to her casual attitude toward sex activities, but also her willingness to procure whatever prohibited substances her "clients" desired.

Lucille was not even thirty years old, but looked like a haggard middle-aged woman. Her drug habit had taken its toll over the years and destroyed whatever good looks she might have had. She slouched when she walked, her speech was often slurred and she was always scratching her itchy skin. As a result, her body was disfigured with streaky scars.

When Jenny was first born, Lucille carried her home in a basket donated by the charity hospital. She took care of her child for a few years, but her drug use overtook her good intentions and suppressed her natural mothering instincts to the point where she no longer cared.

Lucille now lived her life strictly for her own desires. Jenny was neglected and often abandoned for several days. Left alone, the child's only diversion from the misery in her life was provided by a small black and white television set in the corner of the kitchen. A wire coat hanger served as an antenna and a snowy, fuzzy picture from the city's only T.V. station provided a glimpse of the outside world.

Jenny was undernourished and small for her age. She walked around the apartment in a thin cotton dress and socks that needed mending. Her underwear was changed only occasionally and rarely washed. Any washing was done in the kitchen sink with a bar of soap pilfered by Lucille from the tavern. There were no laundry facilities in the tenement building and public laundromats cost money.

A stumbling noise on the outside stairway alerted the dozing girl to her mother's arrival. A suppressed giggle and a man's rasping voice told her that she was not alone.

"Watch your step, Harold," she heard her mother say, "there's a loose mat around here somewhere and a skinny kid to fall over." She grabbed Harold's arm to stop from falling. "The kid is always in the way and sneaks around a lot."

"I didn't know you had a kid," Harold said, "I thought we were gonna be alone, baby. And where's the stuff you promised me?"

"Hold your horses, Harold, I'll get it. And don't you worry about the kid. She'll stay out of the way." Turning to Jenny, she glared at her and added, "If she knows what's good for her."

Jenny slunk to the corner of the kitchen and sat down in front of the T.V. She bent her head down and tried to make herself look even smaller than she was already. Her stomach rumbled to protest its emptiness.

Lucille admonished her, "Now don't you bother us or make a nuisance. Stay put. Get it?" With that she grabbed

Harold hand and dragged him into the bedroom. "We can have a good time in here," she said.

"Is that where the stuff is?" Harold asked, "I think I'm comin' down and need a boost. You look a bit jittery too."

"All in here, baby. Did you bring the money? You gotta give that up front, like I told you. I gotta pay the candy man for it in the morning."

"Yeah, yeah, I got it."

Jenny couldn't hear any more except for mumbled sounds and, afterwards, the familiar creaking of the bed springs. She pulled her dress a little tighter and resigned herself to the rejection by her mother.

- - - - - - - - -

Several streets over, in a more upscale section of town, tall apartment buildings dominated the cityscape. On the second floor of one of the buildings, an argument was taking place. A man, obviously inebriated and still carrying a whiskey bottle in his hand, yelled at a woman, whose dress was torn and stained. "I don't want to hurt you, Emily, but you're making me. I told you a thousand times to leave my stuff alone, but no, you don't listen. What were you trying to do anyways? Spy on me?"

"I was only looking for a pen or a pencil to write the grocery list, Bill. My pen quit working. I think it ran out of ink."

"Oh, yeah? You'd better not have gotten into my private bureau drawers. I don't want you to rummage through them . . . ever! If you dare to defy my orders, you'll face the consequ . . . " He stumbled over the word and finished with, ". . . you'll pay the price!"

"But Bill, did you have to hit me so hard? And look at my dress," Emily wailed.

"Well, sew it up already! You know how to sew, don't you?" With that, Bill stumbled to the bedroom, taking his bottle with him.

Emily looked at her dress. It had been mended many times and was years out of style. She murmured, "Most women now wear slacks and tops, but Bill won't let me buy any of those." She'd heard him say, "You know how to sew, don't you?" so many times, she was sick and tired of it. But she felt powerless to do anything about it.

Emily sank down in a living room chair. Her dress rode up as she sat down and revealed scars from previous abuses by her husband. Her hair was disheveled and her eyes looked tired and were wet with tears.

"Why is he like that to me?" she pondered. "Ever since he came home from work tonight he's been after me. I guess I shouldn't have gone through his things to look for a pen. Maybe he's right to punish me. He does have a right to his privacy."

She shifted in her seat. "But it isn't right for him to abuse me. To hit me and punch me. And what was it I saw in his bureau? Maybe that explains the mysterious phone calls he gets. The late nights. He could be in serious trouble. Maybe I ought to help him. And I would, If he'd let me."

She continued to reflect, "When we were first married, almost ten years ago now, I was happy. He was such a looker! Tall and strong and everyone loved him. I considered myself lucky to marry him. All my friends were envious."

She sighed. "But then the drinking started. At first, a glass of wine at supper. I liked that. It was something we did together. But when he switched to whiskey, he seemed to need that all the time. I couldn't drink whiskey. I don't like the taste of the stuff. But Bill! He joined the drinking crowd. Every day after work he joined them. Didn't come home 'till the supper was cold and I had to heat it up for him. Even then, he ate very little of it. Sometimes none of it."

She pulled her dress a little closer around herself and straightened out the hem. "He was good to me at first. We had fun together. But lately . . . We haven't been close for many years now. He has other interests, other friends, some of them women. I think he has a woman he drinks with and God knows what else . . . "

Her reverie was suddenly interrupted by Bill bursting through the bedroom door, some papers in his hand and a furious look on his face.

"Did you go through my drawers to look for this, you bitch? Somebody went through my stuff. I can tell. What did you see? Did you find these?" He waved the papers in the air. "Who told you to spy on me? If you ever tell anybody about this, I'll kill you . . . !" He shook with rage.

Emily had a glimmer of an idea what he was talking about. When she was looking for a pen, she saw some papers marked as "import documents" and "customs declarations". At the time she thought that they had something to do with Bill's work at the plant where he worked as a shipper. But judging by Bill's reaction, there was obviously something a lot more sinister going on. Possibly something illegal.

Bill strode over to Emily, who had risen from her chair. He grabbed her by the shoulder and shook her violently. "Speak up, woman. I know you saw them. Spill it! Who put you up to this?" He slapped her in the face and punched her in the side. "Did you talk to the cops?"

As Emily screamed with pain, he became more and more angry and threw her back in the chair. She landed on her side, but not in the chair. She missed it by several feet and, after glancing off its arms, crashed on the edge of the coffee table. The table broke and she crumpled to the floor beside the shattered pieces. Moaning with pain, she looked up at Bill.

"I don't know what you're talking about," she said through her tears, "I know nothing about those papers and I've never talked to the police. I wouldn't do that. Please Bill, I'm your wife. I never hurt you. I never would. Please stop hurting me."

Bill, glaring at her, snarled, "Get outta my sight, you bitch! I can't trust you. Just get out! I'm tired of you. You're dull. You're ugly! Just get out, before I throw you out!"

"But where will I go, Bill? It's getting late and it's cold out. It's December and they're calling for snow."

"I don't give a damn! Just get out! I don't want you anywhere near me. When I get back you'd better not be here, or else!"

He turned around abruptly, walked back to the bedroom and slammed the door.

Emily scrambled back on the chair. She sat there, shaking, for several minutes. "Does he really want me to go outside into the cold," she wondered. He had been furious with her and very specific. Her heart ached about the way he had yelled at her. She had a sharp pain in her side and her whole body was sore.

Emily knew that Bill had meant every word. Every insult he had hurled at her. He was obviously convinced that she had betrayed him or would do so at the first opportunity. Staying in the apartment with him was dangerous. He would not hesitate to do her serious harm.

She decided that she had no choice. She had to leave. For a few minutes she thought about calling the police but then concluded that, if Bill found out, it could be her death sentence.

"Perhaps he would calm down a little if I did leave and stayed away for a while," she thought, "Perhaps he would start to worry about me and regret that he treated me so badly." But she knew that was wishful thinking.

She went to the hallway and looked in the closet for her coat. It had been a warm winter coat once. Now worn out and threadbare, the coat was almost twenty years old. She'd bought it when working at an insurance company when she was only in her teens. Bill had never been willing to give her enough money to buy a new one.

With a sigh, she slipped into the coat and put on a pair of gloves. With a last look at the bedroom, she resolutely opened the door and walked down the stairs into the street. At that time of night it was devoid of people or traffic.

Emily walked without purpose. She was all alone. When she came to the Morrison bridge over the Green Valley river, she hesitated. Walking to the railing, she looked down at the dark water reflecting the glow of the street lamps. The water flowed gently and she started wondering what it would feel like if she were to jump into it. Being enveloped appealed to her. Even the water might feel good around her.

"It would serve him right," she thought, "being confronted with a drowned wife would be just punishment for him." The feeling became overpowering and she moved closer to the railing. "I could easily climb up and all I'd have to do is let go."

She looked down again and the water seemed to beckon her. "Come to me," it seemed to say, "In oblivion you'll find peace."

She saw something floating by. It looked like a dead rat. Or perhaps it was a small cat, cruelly discarded by an uncaring person tired of feeding it.

She climbed on the railing ready to commit herself, but then she had a closer look at the dead animal drifting by. It had obviously been in its watery grave for some time, because it had partially decomposed. She imagined herself in that condition and hesitated. The sight in the water filled her with revulsion and she climbed down again.

Resuming her walk, she left the bridge behind and trudged forward. A cold wind came up and chilled her. Snow started to fall and was driven by the wind into her face. Shielding her face with her hands, she walked on. Before long, her hands went numb inside her gloves. She stopped at a tree to catch her breath. She pressed her hands to her aching side, but it didn't do much to relieve the pain.

After a while she resumed her aimless walk, leaving the streetlights behind. She walked into a section of town unfamiliar to her. Dark tenement buildings loomed to her right. A wrecking yard full of broken cars and trucks was to her left. "Broken down, just like me," she reflected.

On and on she walked. Without purpose and without care.

- - - - - - - - -

I seemed like ages before Jenny's mother came out of the bedroom. Over her shoulder, she yelled, "Come on, Harold. Up and at them! Fun's over. Your fifty bucks only goes so far, you know!"

Jenny stirred from her lethargy. "I'm hungry, Mommy. Did you bring me something?"

Lucille frowned. "No, I didn't get a chance. Wasn't there something in the 'frig?"

"Just a piece of cheese, Mommy. But I'm still hungry."

'My purse is here somewhere, kid. Look around for it. I snatched some crackers and mints from the bar." She plopped down on the couch, as Harold stumbled out of the bedroom, still fastening his trousers. She looked at him with disgust. "You look like hell, Harold. You're using too much of the stuff, you know."

"You should talk," Harold replied, "You're at it more'n me. Look at you!"

"Oh, get out of here. Fun's over, like I said. See you around."

As Harold left, Jenny dragged a chair to the kitchen counter and retrieved the purse Lucille had tossed there. "I see some crackers in here, Mommy." She fished out some blister packs with Chinese writing on them. "And are these the mints you talked about?"

Lucille jumped up and grabbed the purse from Jenny's hands. "No, leave them alone. They're mine." She thrust the crackers at her daughter. "I guess I didn't get any mints. You'll have to be happy with these crackers."

She rummaged through her purse. "I know I got . . . What was it he called it? Oh yeah, Fentanyl lozenges. They're supposed to be really something. Don't know if you're supposed to take them whole or chew them. I'll do one of each."

She walked to the sink and poured some water in a cup. She separated the foil of one of the blister packs, swallowed one of the lozenges and then chewed a second one.

"Nothing," she mumbled. "No kick whatsoever. Probably been cut to add to the profits." She popped another lozenge in her mouth and stretched out on the couch,

Jenny finished the last of her cracker meal and climbed up beside her mother, snuggling close for a little warmth and went to sleep.

Lucille's breathing gradually slowed and became sporadic. She started to sweat and her face paled. She snored unevenly but was not asleep. Her pupils slowly became pinpoints. She tried to get up but was unable to do so. She sank back on the couch in a limp heap. Her skin showed blue and ashen patches and then her breathing stopped altogether. A few minutes later she was dead.

- - - - - - - - -

Her worst hunger pangs having subsided, Jenny slept for almost two hours. She was shivering when she awoke. Her mother had been warm when she first crawled against her, but now she felt cool.

"Mommy, wake up," Jenny urged her, "I'm so cold. And I'm still hungry."

Getting no response, Jenny shook her mother's arm, but it was slack and dropped off the couch. Jenny started to panic and burst into tears. "Mommy, wake up! There's no heat and I'm hungry." She knew instinctively that something serious had happened and that she needed help.

She went to the coat hooks on the kitchen wall and tried to get her coat, but couldn't reach it. She dragged a chair over and climbed on. Still having trouble removing the coat from the hook, she tugged on it as hard as she could and tore off the loop at its collar. As the coat came loose, she tumbled down to the floor with it.

Gritting her teeth against the pain, the little girl put on her coat and her slip-on canvass shoes with the duck decoration – a gift from the Salvation Army some time ago. The shoes were a little tight but they were the only footwear she had.

Casting one last look at her lifeless mother, she opened the door and descended the stairs, She had no idea where to go for help, but she set out bravely down the street.

The night was very dark and there were no people about. She walked for several blocks until she became tired and looked for a place to rest. Finding none, she sat down on a large log at the edge of a church parking lot and cried piteously. She was very cold and the swirling snow bit into her face. It seemed to cut right through her flimsy coat. She laid down on the log and pulled up her tiny legs into a fetal position.

Emily had been walking non-stop for more than two miles. She was getting very tired and looked for a place to rest for a while. All she could see were dark foreboding buildings and scrap yards. But there was a church a few blocks ahead and she hoped to find refuge from the cold there. But when she tried the massive door, it was locked.

Looking around for a place to rest, she saw a log at the edge of the parking lot and walked over to it. A small pile of what looked like a bundle of discarded clothes was at one end of the log. When she got closer, she discovered that it was a small child, in worse condition than she was. She picked it up. It was a little girl, weighing no more than a sack of groceries.

"Oh my God," she cried out, "what are you doing here? You must be freezing cold!"

Receiving only a moan in reply, she took off her coat and wrapped the child in it.

"You're as cold and lost as I am," she said, "We'll rest a little while and then I'll carry you to safety." She sat down on the log and hugged the child as though it were her own – a little child she had not ever been able to hold or love. Not when her husband wanted nothing to do with what he considered to be a "bloody nuisance".

The temperature continued to drop. The wind became a sharp-edged sword, cutting through Emily's flimsy dress and numbing her body. The little girl's breathing was becoming erratic and she hugged her closer to her bosom.

Emily shivered violently. The snow was coming down heavier and seemed to attack her, swirling and rushing at her straight on. She slumped down, unable to resist the onslaught.

It wasn't long before the heap of humanity, that was Emily and little Jenny, stilled and became unrecognizable as anything other that a pile of thrown away trash in the snow.

But that was not the end. As Emily's limbs stiffened and her extremities turned blue due to frostbite, she no longer felt the cold. Her exhausted muscles started to relax and a feeling of warmth coursed throughout her body.

Not realizing that this was the result of hypothermia, Emily tried to get up, but was unable to do so. She wrapped her coat more closely around the child and began to hallucinate.

Being so close to Christmas, she imagined a host of angels beckoning her and the child to follow them up into the blue. A feeling of awe and excitement came over her. Loneliness and neglect melted like snow from the rooftops in Spring and she felt closer to Heaven than ever before. She was no longer an abused wife who had come across an abandoned child. They were being welcomed as cherished children of God.

She had visions of a peaceful meadow with grazing sheep and friendly shepherds. A meadow with stars by the million overhead where large sheepdogs guarded the flock and she and the little girl were part of that flock, protected and shielded from harm..

She could almost feel the dogs' presence and hear the snuffling sounds they made. In her vision, a shepherd called to one of the dogs. "What are you doing, Rufus? What did you find? Don't go rooting around in the trash."

She didn't understand that last part and, with great effort, opened her eyes. What she saw astounded and delighted her. A man, holding the leash of a large dog, brushed the snow off her face and, talking in an excited voice, yelled, "Glory be! It's a woman, half frozen and with a little child!"

The man fumbled in his pocket and produced a cell phone. "Wait 'till I call 9 1 1. What possessed you to go to sleep on a log and in this neighbourhood of all places?"

Emily held on tightly to the child and refused to let go of it, so he gently laid both of them flat on the log, took off his winter coat and covered them just as the ambulance arrived. He introduced himself as Rev. Christopher Walker to the paramedics and rode with them to the hospital. There, he put Rufus in charge of an orderly and settled himself in the waiting room with a hot cup of coffee. The police were called and he told them of his late night discovery.

It was more than three hours before the doctor told him that they had been successful in reviving their patients by carefully and slowly warming them with fluids and restoring their internal temperature. However, it would be several days before they could be discharged.

Walker thanked him, retrieved Rufus and promised to return in the morning.

- - - - - - - - -

It was almost two days before Emily was able to give a full account of finding Jenny on the log, slowly freezing to death. It was a miracle that the little girl survived at all. Being so small, she was subject to being chilled much faster than a full grown person, because of the relatively large skin surface to body mass ratio.

But careful and loving handling by the hospital's nurses was successful and, other than a slight handicap in the use of her left hand, she recovered completely. Being called a "miracle baby" by the newspapers, she was the darling of the hospital staff and Emily was her biggest fan.

Emily, too, recovered nicely and was soon ready to be discharged. But she did not want to go home. Her uncaring and abusive husband had not even come to see her during her hospital stay. Emily hoped that it was because he was ashamed of his mistreatment of her, but, more likely, he felt the burden of the assault charges leveled against him by the authorities.

Being empathetic with Emily's predicament, Rev. Walker offered to take Emily and Jenny to his home. "I have a loving, caring wife and a wonderful little daughter just about Jenny's age. We would love to have the two of you spend the Christmas Holidays with us. Stay at least until after New Year's day. In the meantime we will try to find a permanent solution," he said.

The Walker family, with Emily and Jenny as their guests, enjoyed a wonderful Christmas celebration. Jenny and Walker's daughter, whose name was Melinda, quickly became friends and were inseparable throughout the holidays.

After battling much red tape and, with the help of Rev. Walker's church members, Emily obtained a divorce from her husband. She became an apprentice social worker in the city, specializing in elder care for lonely seniors. Her kind and friendly personality stood her in good stead and she loved her job.

Eventually, her happiness became complete with the adoption of Jenny as her own little girl.

THE END

THE MIRACLE

by

Arie Van der Ende

When the blast of war blows in our ears, (we) imitate the tiger.

Stiffen the sinews, summon up the blood.

Disguise fair nature with hard-favour'd rage.

Shakespeare, Henry V. 1564 - 1616.

Older men declare war. But it is youth that must fight and die.

Herbert Hoover. 1874 - 1964.

In war, whichever side may call itself the victor,

there are no winners, but all are losers.

Neville Chamberlin. 1869 – 1940.

Bram van Dorp was careful to creep silently through the swamp. If he were to attract attention to his presence, it could mean his life. After all, he had aligned himself with a group of saboteurs and was on his way to rendezvous with them. They were to discuss plans for the derailment of a train.

It was March, 1944 and the German occupation forces did not take kindly to saboteurs. They were especially vigilant about their train schedule.

It started to get dark. A low mist hung over the land and a stinging rain made shallow puddles on the ground. His clothes were muddy and he was cold. Low thorny bushes were scratching him and stands of stinging nettles dotted the terrain. It was difficult to move without making some noise. His body ached and he had to rest frequently. When he did, he listened intently for any sounds that might present a danger to him.

The rain finally stopped and a chill wind started.

He peered around a bramble bush to get his bearings. A wooden gate, where the group had agreed to meet, was about a quarter mile ahead.

He was just about to crawl forward again, when he heard a sound. It was coming from his left. Another person was making his way towards the same destination. An enemy? Or, perhaps, a fellow saboteur? He couldn't tell, but he couldn't take a chance either.

His fellow traveller was slowly catching up with him, still to his left. He steeled himself and just as the man drew even with him, he sprang, landing on top of his quarry. He placed his left hand across the man's mouth and his right in the back of his neck. Speaking in a hoarse whisper, he growled, "Don't make a sound or I'll break your neck."

Wisely the man kept quiet. Bram could tell that he was only slightly built and could be easily overpowered. At age 19, Bram was almost six feet tall and well muscled. He pinched the man's neck more tightly and whispered, "What are you doing here? Are you following me? Speak, but speak softly."

His adversary went limp but then, with a lithe movement, turned over and wrenched himself clear. Bram felt a sudden agonizing stab of pain as he was kicked viciously. He had lost all advantage of surprise.

To his astonishment, he heard a female voice say, "Sorry for that kick but I didn't want you to break my neck."

"You . . . you're a girl," Bram stammered, "A young one at that. Who are you? What's your name?" He couldn't see her very well in the dark, but reached out and grabbed her by the shoulders to prevent her from escaping.

The girl resisted his grip. She wiggled her body but was unable to escape his hold, so she stopped struggling and said, "You can let go. I won't try to get away. I'm part of your group. I was on my way to link up with you at that gate up yonder. Anything to resist the rotmoffen."

Rotmoffen. The common term for the hated occupation forces in Holland. Over the past four years they had wreaked havoc on the country. Holland, once prosperous and one of the wealthiest trading nations in Europe, had been robbed and defiled by the German army to the point of not having enough resources left to feed its population. The country had been systematically looted in order to replenish Germany's depleted reserves.

"Glad you're with us," Bram said, "My name is . . . "

The girl punched him and whispered, "No, don't tell me your name. Names are dangerous and traceable. And they are unnecessary. I'll just call you 'Joe'. Use that as your name from now on."

"And you? What'll I call you?"

"How about 'Merry', as in Merry Christmas? By Christmastime I hope our country will be free from this madness."

Bram, now renamed Joe, said, "O.K., Merry it is."

"Enough chit-chat, Joe. We have an appointment to keep. Let's carry on." With that she turned around abruptly and started to crawl towards the gate.

Joe followed her, but they had not gone more than ten feet when the sudden blaze of a searchlight pierced the darkness and a rough German voice rang out, "Halt! Haende hoch! - - Stop! Hands up! - Oder werden wir schiessen! - Or we'll shoot!"

Merry stirred to comply, but Joe pushed her down forcibly and plopped down beside her in the muddy water of a deep depression behind a bush. "Keep your eyes tightly closed," he whispered, "otherwise the light will reflect in your pupils and you'll give us away."

He had barely finished speaking when the rat-tat-tat of a machine gun echoed through the still of the night and two of three men at the gate clutched their chest and fell down. The third raised his arms to surrender and, with a trembling voice, pleaded, "What are you doing? You promised no violence if I told you what we were planning. You said we would be punished only slightly if I told you everything and no actual harm was done." His voice carried and Joe and Merry could easily hear every word. They depressed their bodies even deeper into the mud.

"I was promise you dat, nichtwar?" The German sergeant spoke with a broken accent. "I lied." Turning to the soldiers beside him, he barked, "Erschiessen Sie ihn auch - Shoot him too!" The sergeant obviously hated traitors, whether from his own side or the enemy's. More shots rang out.

The Germans searched the area and came very close to discovering Joe and Merry. When one of the soldiers almost stepped on them, it was excruciatingly difficult for Joe and Merry to keep their eyes closed, but they managed to do so.

The sergeant instructed his soldiers to drag the dead bodies to a truck parked nearby and then to 'string them up, upside down, on lamp posts in town as a warning to the town's people'.

After the soldiers had left, Joe and Merry finally dared to move. Merry was shivering and not just from the cold. "Let's get out of here, Joe, quick!"

Joe put his arm around Merry and said, "We have just gone through a traumatic experience. We have observed the brutal murder of our comrades. It is now up to the two of us to find a way to derail that train."

Merry asked, "Why are we doing that?"

Joe said, "Late yesterday all four Jewish families in town, including their children, were arrested, just because they are Jews. Some of them have lived here all their lives, but the Germans hate them. I don't know why. A few years ago they made them wear a bright yellow star on their clothes, but now they want to ship them to concentration camps deep in Germany. There have been reports of mass murder in those camps. We found out that they are to be shipped by freight train early tomorrow morning. We intent to stop that train and rescue them. There are people standing by to take them in and hide them."

Merry looked at Joe doubtfully. "Would they really murder them? The children too?"

"I'm afraid so, Merry. It seems that the whole world has gone mad."

"At what time is that train scheduled to leave?"

"At four o'clock in the morning. So we'll need to leave here no later than two hours before that."

Merry continued to shiver. Joe said, "We need to get out of these wet clothes or we'll catch pneumonia. The rain has stopped but we're chilled to the bone. We need to get some dry clothes and I know just where to get them."

He led Merry to an isolated farmhouse. He said, "I know the people who live here. They have a daughter about your size and the man is about the size of me. His wife always does her laundry on Mondays and hangs her clothes on a clothesline strung across their yard. When it rains, as it did today, she leaves them hanging there and lets the night breeze dry them They don't have a dog to alert them, so we'll 'liberate' what we need."

Joe explained that he and his fellow conspirators had intended to hide in a nearby barn until the appointed hour. "Now that place may be compromised. We don't know how much the traitor has told the moffen, but we can't take a chance. I am familiar with this area and I know of a place where we can hole up safely for a few hours. It's a small shed used for storing farm implements."

"But we need to wash off this mud first," Merry said.

"You're right, of course," Joe answered, "and we'll do that in the creek that runs next to the tool shed."

After another half mile, they arrived at their destination.

"The water will be cold, but not as cold as this night air. Let's jump in fully clothed and rinse off as much of the mud as we can and then we'll put on the dry clothes in the shed."

Joe found some jute sacks and a tarp, with which he covered Merry, who was still shivering. The clothes they had obtained barely fit Joe, but were just the right size for Merry.

"I think we'll be safe here for a few hours," Joe said, "but we'll need to leave here at around two o'clock."

"As long as I can get a few hours rest, I should be O.K." Merry said as she snuggled down. "but I'm still so cold!"

Joe laid down beside her and cradled her in his arms.

"Mm. I feel safe with you, Joe," Merry purred, "you hold me just as my Daddy used to."

"How old are you anyways, Merry, you look only about fourteen," Joe said.

"I'm older than that! Next month will be my seventeenth birthday! It's just that I'm small for my age."

"Well, you're very brave to do what you're doing. Not many young girls would dare it. What made you join the resistance movement?"

"When Germany invaded Holland in 1940, both my parents were killed." Merry suppressed a sob. "I've been living with my aunt since then." Looking up defiantly, she added, "I want to get back at those German moffen for what they did."

Putting her arm around Joe's waist, she whispered, "Hold me closer, Joe. You feel so nice and warm."

Joe pulled her body to his and a surge of tenderness flowed through him. As they lay there, together, the warm feeling expanded and blossomed into passion. Being young and impulsive, their hormone-fueled desires took over and, before long, they found orgasmic release from the tensions of the past few hours. They dosed off, secure in each other's arms until Joe awoke, with a start.

"Merry, wake up, sweetheart, it's time for us to go."

Merry stirred slowly. "I had the most amazing dream," she said, "you and I walked down the aisle of a cathedral and . . ." She stopped suddenly and her cheeks flushed. "Oh, Joe, did we . . . " She looked at Joe shyly.

"Merry, dear, sweet Merry. I've fallen deeply in love with you. I want to protect you always. I want you to stay here, where you're safe, while I try to finish the job we started." He spread his arms protectively.

Merry squared her shoulders. "No way, Joe. That's not going to happen. I'm with you all the way. You're not going to exclude me. I'm coming."

"But Merry, I would never forgive myself if you got hurt," Joe protested.

"Listen, you idiot, I'd rather spend one hour with you doing dangerous work than spend a lifetime worrying about what might happen or what might have been. Don't you understand that, sweetheart?"

Joe gave in, reluctantly, seeing that there was no changing her mind.

Picking up a crow bar and a nail puller from the stash of tools in the shed, Joe said, "Here are some things we can use to stop that train. Let's take these and be on our way. Are you ready?"

- - - - - - - - -

When Joe and Merry arrived at the section of track chosen for derailment, they found about 15 resistance fighters there. A large number of rail spikes had already been pulled and it did not take long to remove two lengths of track.

When the task was completed, they reviewed the plan of attack and settled down to wait. They lapsed into a somber silence, anticipating the battle to come. They didn't have long to wait.

The train approached the curve in the dark. It consisted of a locomotive, a cattle car holding the unfortunate Jewish prisoners, and a caboose, sporting a mounted machine gun and loaded with explosives. There were six soldiers with it, two with the machine gun, two in the front and two inside.

The train slowed down for the curve. The engineer couldn't see that a portion of the track was missing and as the train speeded up again, it reached the sabotaged section. A loud thump accompanied the drop off the track, there was a piercing shriek as the train wheels protested the sudden change in direction, and the locomotive slid down the embankment. It carried the rest of the train with it.

Screams could be heard coming from the cattle car blending with curses from the caboose. The machine gun broke off and the soldiers were thrown from the train. They were seasoned troops, however, and immediately started firing at the saboteurs.

They killed a half dozen of them right away, But they were outnumbered and the well-armed resistance fighters killed them all. The engineer and his assistant were also quickly dispatched and the prisoners were released. The ammunition in the caboose was taken by the resistance for later use.

The Jewish people, which included six children, were spirited away.

Merry and Joe left.

- - - - - - - - - - -

After again spending the night in their tool shed hide-a-way, Joe and Merry decided to walk to the next town. The sooner they left the area, the better they would avoid being arrested. They talked of love and marriage.

"As far as I'm concerned," said Joe, "I consider you to be my wife. As long as this mad war is dragging on, a formal wedding is impossible. All males from 18 to 45 are required to work as forced labour. That compels me to be an 'onderduiker' - an underground resistance fighter."

The German search net had been cast much wider than they had anticipated. The following morning, as they were walking, a halftrack stopped beside them and they were taken to a German interrogation centre.

When the half dozen soldiers in the barracks saw Merry, they started to drool and make lewd remarks. When Joe objected and told them to "leave my wife alone", they tied him to a post in the corner of the room.

They shoved Merry around from one soldier to another, pawing her and attempting to kiss her. Merry fought like a tigress, punching and scratching, but that only served to egg them on.

A large corporal grabbed her and wrestled her to the floor. Laughing and swearing, a few of his buddies held her down while he spread her legs. Joe yelled and screamed, but his bonds held him fast and he was forced to watch while the corporal clawed at Merry's underwear. The other men shouted encouragement and yelled for him to "hurry up", so they could have a turn.

Joe struggled and pleaded and cajoled, but it was no use. Merry fought and spit and bit, but the best she could do was minor damage. With her arms and legs held by three strong men, she could only struggle in vain.

Relief from her agony finally came from an unexpected quarter. The door opened and a colonel entered. At first, the soldiers didn't see him and even after two of the men jumped up and yelled "Achtung!", the corporal continued raping Merry. Not until the colonel barked, "Was ist denn hier los? - What's going on here?" did the corporal recover from his lust-filled behaviour and made a feeble attempt to rise to his feet.

What was "going on here" was self-evident. The colonel could see Merry crying on the floor, her dress hiked above her waist and her underwear in disarray. To the corporal he snarled, "Aufstehen! - get up!"

The brute achieved an unsteady vertical position and mumbled, "Ja, herr Oberst - yes, colonel." The colonel looked at him in disgust, "Du schmutziges Schwein! Ich werde Sie spaeter behandeln. Raus! - you filthy swine! I'll deal with you later. Get out!"

The colonel made one of the men untie Joe, who went immediately to help Merry.

Addressing Joe, the colonel said, "I apologize for the disgusting behaviour of my men. Not all Germans are like that. I assure you that they will be punished. There is nothing more I can do. Please leave and stay well away from here."

With a pained look on his face, he continued, " This miserable war is causing great moral decline and obscene behaviour. Again, I promise that my men will be punished."

- - - - - - - - - - -

After stopping at a drug store for some medication, Joe led Merry back to the tool shed and made her lie down and rest. Merry was very quiet and had a vacant look in her eyes. The ordeal had shaken her badly. Her body had been grossly violated.

It wasn't that Merry had been a virgin. Like many teenagers, there had been a few occasions when she had succumbed to her natural needs and desires. But that had been **her** choice. Just as it had been her choice to surrender herself to Joe during their "tool shed love". That had involved tenderness and love and caring.

What happened in the German barracks was a brutal attack. Rape. Assault. Raw, primal and overpowering. It turned the sex act from intimate, shared love into something dirty and repulsive.

Joe did his best to comfort her. He assured her of his continuing love and respect. Time and again he told her that his love for her would last forever. That she had nothing to be ashamed of. That the deed was done **to** her - not **by** her. He tried to persuade her to push the ordeal into the background and go on with her life.

Merry burst out crying and put her head on Joe's shoulder. Her body heaved and she hugged Joe, hanging on to him for support. Joe stroked her blonde hair and whispered encouraging words to her. Finally, when Merry was cried out, she fell asleep and Joe gently covered her with the tarp. He laid down beside her and cradled her in his arms until daybreak.

By morning Merry seemed to feel better. She hugged Joe and thanked him for his encouragement. She said, "You are right, Joe. I can't bury myself in self-pity. There is a war going on and we have a job to do. To get over this we must continue to resist the German occupiers and help prepare our country for eventual liberation from this nightmare."

- - - - - - - - - - -

During the next several weeks, Merry and Joe travelled from town to town and joined several local resistance units on a temporary basis. They sabotaged equipment, disrupted troop movements and caused general mischief to the Germans. Unless absolutely necessary, they avoided the killing of German soldiers, not only because it didn't "feel right to them", but also because it invariable led to reprisals.

They found shelter in the many agricultural buildings dotting the land. Holland is densely populated and the towns are close together, so they found plenty of places to hide. Surreptitious assistance was difficult for the Germans to detect and almost impossible to prevent, so, generally, many people were willing to assist them with a meal here and there, an offer of shelter or a change of clothes.

One morning, Merry was slow to get started . When Joe urged her to hurry up, Merry said, "Joe, darling, it's not that I don't want to go, but I'm so tired this morning. " She was about to explain, when Joe interrupted her and said, "Merry, I understand. We've been going at it without stopping for several weeks now. Perhaps we need to rest for a day or two."

Merry said, "Joe, it's more than that. I think I know what's wrong with me." She burst out crying. "Oh, Joe, that nasty brute who raped me . . . I think he impregnated me. . . " She shuddered and looked helplessly at Joe. "What are we . . . "

Joe put his arms around her and said, " I was born in this town. There's only one doctor here and I know him well. Let's go and see him. He's a nice man. Let's ask him for advice. Come on, sweetheart, dry your tears."

Avoiding the main roads, they arrived at the doctor's house and knocked at his back door. The housekeeper answered and said, "Sorry, Dr. Van Vliet is just having his breakfast. Can you come back in about an hour?" She stopped suddenly and took a closer look at Joe. "Are you the

Van Dorp boy? How you've grown! Are you in trouble? You must be. Come in and get something to eat. What do you want to see Dr. Van Vliet about? Is there something I can help you with?"

"No, we need to see the doctor," Joe replied, "We need his advice."

The housekeeper nodded. "I'll go and fetch him. Wait here and have some of those biscuits. Made fresh this morning."

The doctor entered the kitchen. He was an old man, though only in his sixties. He was slightly stooped and had silver hair. His glasses had slipped to the end of his nose and his face was wrinkled. He adjusted his tie and said, "Did I hear right? Young Van Dorp is here?" He looked Joe up and down and remarked, "You've grown some since I last saw you. And whom do we have here?" he added, looking at Merry. He nodded his approval. "You always could pick the pretty ones."

"This is Merry, doctor, she's my wife."

"Well, well, . . . congratulations, my boy," the doctor said. He looked inquiringly at Joe. "What is the problem you need help with? You look in good shape. But I suppose you have gone underground?"

"Doctor, we need your help. You see, Merry believes she may be pregnant."

"Again, congratulations." But then a crease covered his forehead and he added, "But this may not be the best time to bring up a child. This war . . . "

Joe interrupted, "Doctor, we need to talk. There's a lot more to it". He looked to the doctor's study down the hall.

Dr. Van Vliet took the hint. "Let's go into my study and you can tell me all about it."

After Joe had explained the rape in the German barracks, Dr. Van Vliet said, "Let me ask some questions. Some of them are very personal, but the answers are important. First off, if you, young lady, are indeed pregnant, are you now looking to end that pregnancy? In that case we would be entering dangerous and illegal territory and you came to the wrong place. I am a doctor and have sworn to preserve life, not destroy it." He looked sternly at them.

Joe jumped in. "But doctor, Merry was raped. That surely must make a difference! An abortion at this early stage and under these circumstances should surely be morally justified!"

"I am not arguing the point, son. But the law of the land makes it a crime and I won't do it."

Merry, who had been silent until then, spoke up. With tears in her eyes, she stomped her foot and said, "You didn't ask **me**! I am the one carrying a baby! A baby who's not even born yet. A baby who's not to blame for anything. A baby who has the right to its life. I won't agree to end that life!"

Joe looked surprised. He sputtered, "But . . . but Merry . . ."

"Please Joe, I love you and I know how you feel, but this is my body and my decision. I've thought and worried about this all last night and this is what I want. It is what I feel is right. Please understand, sweetheart."

Joe hugged her and whispered, "I love you Merry. More than I can say. And I understand. I'll stand by your decision. No matter what."

While the two lovers were talking and hugging, the doctor smiled and said, "I'm glad that's settled. But now, let's carry on. As I said before, there are several questions I want to ask. In the first place, let's make sure you actually **are** pregnant.

About 15 years ago a scientist in South Africa, by the name of Lancelot Hogben, developed a test to detect a hormone present only in a woman who is pregnant. I can do that test today and have the results by tonight."

"What kind of test is that, doctor? I don't want Merry hurt." Joe said, looking worried. "Now that we have decided to keep the baby, I want Merry treated with special care."

"Son, it is a myth that pregnant women should be considered fragile. It is true that they should receive nourishing food, regular medical care and understanding, but childbirth is a natural thing and women are quite capable of carrying out the task. Just show her your love and realize that major changes in her body and in her moods will take place."

The doctor added, "As regards the test, we are looking for human chorionic gonadotropin or the hCG hormone. It requires a small amount of urine and a frog."

"A frog? You're kidding aren't you, doc?"

"I rarely kid, son. The urine is injected into a special type of frog. If the woman is pregnant, the frog begins to lay eggs within a day. The test is quite reliable."

The doctor took Merry into his examination room to do the test. When they came out again, he said, "Merry is in great shape and she'll do just fine. We should know the test result by tonight. Now then, to the rest of the questions. When did the assault take place? Three weeks ago? Exactly what day?"

Merry said, "March 24. I'll never forget that day."

"When did you two first meet?"

The answer came immediately. "Two days before that, March 22. I'll never forget that day either."

The doctor looked at them seriously. "Now comes the delicate question. When did you two first have sexual intercourse? And did you use a condom? I don't mean to pry but this is important."

Joe answered this time. "Doctor, We fell in love the same night we met. And we consummated that love spontaneously and with abandon. You must understand that it was 'love at first sight'. " He continued, "You may be skeptical, but yes, there really is such a thing. I can vouch for it. It really happened."

"I believe you, son. But here's the thing. You seem to be convinced that the supposed pregnancy is the result of the rape. But it may not be. It may be that you two are the parents of the baby Merry is carrying. The fertilization most likely occurred before the rape took place."

Joe almost jumped. "What makes you say that? Could that be? How can you tell? Is there a test for that too?"

"There is a paternity test that compares the blood type of the child with that of the parents, and another one that compares certain proteins in the blood. However, even the best of these tests is not very accurate. Perhaps a more reliable test will be developed in the future. But I base my opinion not on a test, but on a biological fact. To explain it as simply as possible, once a sperm has obtained access to an egg, all other sperm are denied entrance and die."

Looking at Joe, he continued, "So, when you two made unrestrained love, and your sperm joined with Merry's egg, it caused a cortical reaction that blocked any other sperm from gaining entrance, and that would include the sperm of the rapist . Ergo, the baby is most likely the offspring of the two of you."

- - - - - - - - - -

Throughout the summer months, Joe and Merry carried on with their clandestine activities in the underground. They found out that the colonel who had saved Merry from the rapist, had made good on his promise and had demoted the corporal to the rank of private. Shortly after that, the colonel was transferred back to Germany.

The new commandant, however, took advantage of the former corporal's violent personality, promoted him to sergeant and put him in charge of hunting down and executing saboteurs.

The Allies, in September, launched a massive assault in an attempt to cross the Rhine river at Arnhem. a city in the Eastern part of Holland. The week-long operation failed after more than 16,000 lives were lost, as well as causing an estimated 13,000 German casualties.

The Germans retaliated by stopping all food deliveries to the Western part of Holland. As the winter of 1944 - 1945 set in, that decree caused mass starvation in the cities there.

Grocery stores had bouquets of wild flowers in their display windows, but no food on their shelves. Butcher stores were closed. Under penalty of death, farmers were prohibited from providing food to non-Germans, but were forced to hand over all of their crop yields to the occupation forces. People tried to trade their valuables for food. Family pets mysteriously disappeared. Some families painted their daughters' lips and nails and tried to trade their pitiful services for food. At least 22,000 people died from starvation.

Joe and Merry took part in several raids on German food storage buildings and tried to help but with millions of people suffering, that task was next to impossible. They did manage to provide for Merry's growing needs, but a combination of increased German hunting patrols and decreased food supplies forced them to leave the area and head South towards the province of Zeeland.

- - - - - - - - - - -

Zeeland, meaning 'sea - land', is aptly named. The province consists of numerous islands, surrounded by the tidal waters of the North sea and by the delta waters of three major rivers - the Rhine, the Meuse and the Scheldt. These islands, connected by bridges and tunnels, are mainly used for farming and are protected from the angry sea by dikes. The province is in close proximity to Rotterdam, the largest seaport in Europe, as well as to Antwerp in Belgium.

To secure Antwerp as a supply port for the advancing Allied troops, the RAF bombed the precious dikes and flooded the low-lying land to allow for the use of amphibious vehicles. The Southern part of Zeeland was conquered by November at a cost of almost 13,000 casualties, mostly Canadians.

For the local underground there was plenty of opportunity to hinder the German defenses and Joe and

Merry joined in the fight. However, Merry's pregnancy made it necessary to severely restrict her activity.

With the German anti-saboteur patrols in full hunting mode, it became more and more difficult for them to find a safe hiding place. Anyone caught sheltering members of the underground was shot on the spot, so people had become hesitant to help them. Joe and Merry were in constant danger of being discovered and they had to find a different place each night.

Sometimes it was necessary to improvise and make do with a haystack or the bombed-out ruins of a house or barn. Obviously, this was not any way for a pregnant woman to live. It became increasingly impossible and Joe made the decision to curtail their involvement with the underground.

One morning, with Merry's due date fast approaching, they came across a prosperous-looking farm building on one of the islands. Before the war, it had been a bed-and-breakfast operation, as well as a working farm. A sign, which read "Zeeland's Best", was still visible among the neglected shrubs. Joe knocked on the door and when a haggard man answered, inquired about lodgings.

The man, short, stooped and nervous, answered, "No, sorry, we have no room for lodgers. The Germans have taken up all our rooms." He added, "I have no choice, you see. They bring food and they have guns . . . My daughter and I have a hard time looking after them. Sometimes they get drunk and . . . well . . . my daughter is young and they . . . well, they have guns, you see. Please . . . I see that your wife is . . . well . . . I'm really sorry, but you see, you'd better not be seen here . . . "

He was about to shut the door when a young woman in her early twenties pushed him aside. She was tall, had a pretty face and a nubile body. Her pre-war printed dress was at least two sizes too small for her and had ridden up to above her knees. She tugged it down and said to her father, "Daddy, you can't be serious. Can't you see that she's about due? We've got to help them somehow."

"But how can we, Anneke? This man is . . . well, he's . . . being hunted, I can tell. You know what they do to people like him. And they wouldn't stop there. They'd shoot me too and then take you and . . . " He left the rest unsaid, but his meaning was clear.

Anneke replied, "Oh, I know we can't let them stay in the house, but how about the cattle barn? The moffen don't know about that place. It's dry there and sheltered. I can give them some blankets and some food. At least for tonight. We can't just . . . "

The man gave in reluctantly. "Oh, alright, go ahead and take them there. But do it quickly. Those Germans will soon be here for the night."

Anneke grabbed some provisions and led Joe and Merry to several rowboats in the yard. She said, "The fields on our island have been flooded ever since the dikes were bombed, so we have to use boats to get to the barn. It's at the far end of this field. We keep our old horse there and a few sheep. The Germans don't know about it or they would confiscate them. We may have to slaughter the sheep if the food shortage gets worse."

They pushed one of the boats into the surprisingly clear water. Joe took the oars and they rowed to the distant barn which was shrouded in mist. The barn was on a small hill. There was some bomb damage and the roof was partially caved in, but there was a dry section warmed by the animals' body heat.

Merry lay down on some straw next to the sheep Anneke put a few blankets around her and whispered, "I've had some training as a nurse, so I can help you when the baby comes. I'll be back in a few hours but for now I've got to go back and help my father with the Germans." With that she left. Merry listened to the sound of the splashing oars slowly fading away.

Joe snuggled up to Merry, pulled some straw around himself and they dozed off.

About an hour later, they woke with a start when they heard someone scrambling through the barn door. "Anneke came back early," Merry said. She was just about to say something else, when a tall burly German soldier appeared. He seemed as startled as they were and exclaimed, "Was ist los? - What's going on?" He levelled his rifled and pointed it directly at Joe.

Merry gasped and drew the blankets closer to her. "Oh, Joe, please don't fight him. We must think of the baby."

The soldier might not have understood what she said, but he did understand the word 'baby', which is the same in German. He took a closer look at Merry and then his face lit up. He moved a little closer and said, "Waren Sie nicht . . . Oh, ja . . . Verdammt! - Did you not . . .

Oh, yes . . . Dammit!" He lowered his weapon and said with a broken German accent, "Ich was dar as dat Korporal . . . " His speech faltered and he started to stumble over his words. " . . . vergemaltigen . . . angegriffen - . . . rape . . . attacked . . .

" He pointed to Merry's swollen belly. "Das baby . . . ? he asked.

Merry didn't answer. All that summer she had assured herself that the baby was fathered by Joe. But now she realized that, in order to obtain sympathy from this soldier, she should play along with his assumption that the baby was the result of the rape. So she remained silent.

Abruptly, the soldier turned around, walked out of the barn and rowed away.

Shortly after that, they again heard a boat approaching, but this time it was indeed Anneke. She said, "Sorry to be late but I had to wait until that soldier left. Did he discover you or were you able to hide?"

Joe answered, "He did discover us, but he felt sorry for us and left us alone." He added, "Now that you're here, Anneke, I'll leave Merry in your capable hands."

Anneke looked up. "Aren't you going to be here when the baby comes?"

Joe fidgeted, looked embarrassed and said, "I know this is 1944 and we are supposed to live in an enlightened age, but I am old-fashioned and I don't . . . " He added quickly, "If you weren't here, I assure you that I would do anything to help Merry. But you are so much more . . . you're a woman . . .and . . ."

Anneke smiled. "You're embarrassed, aren't you? But you don't need to be. Having a baby is the most natural thing in the world. It happens every day."

"Yes, I know, but, I'm sorry, Anneke, but, as I said, I'm old-fashioned . . . "

Merry spoke up then. "Joe, I understand. But some day fathers will be wanting to witness the miracle of birth. Perhaps next time . . . "

"That's enough," Anneke said, "We've got to get ready. I have some linen here and other stuff Merry will need." She felt Merry's belly. "And it won't be long now."

Merry winced and said, "No, it won't. The contractions are coming regularly now."

There was the sound of a boat approaching. Joe stiffened and whispered, "\somebody's coming. Try to be very quiet." He moved to the barn door.

There were shouts. "Anneke, Anneke, Are you in there?"

"That's my father. What on earth is going on? Why is he shouting? He's going to give us away!"

Again the shouting. "Anneke, where are you?" A boat bumped up against the barn door. "Anneke!"

"Father, be quiet ! You'll alert the Germans!"

"What Germans? They've gone! They've all disappeared! The Canadians are here now! The Germans have left!"

Just then, Merry screamed, followed by the sound of a baby crying. "Anneke," Merry said, with a suppressed squeal of delight. "The baby just slid out, smooth as silk. So easy . . . so slippery . . . Oh, look . . . it's a boy . . . Oh Joe, he's beautiful! . . . Anneke, come see . . . "

For a second Anneke didn't know whether to shush her father, who was obviously in an frenzy or to turn to Merry. She rushed over to Merry, grabbed the baby, and, without bothering with the umbilical cord, laid the baby on Merry's breast and started the task of cleaning.

Joe just stood there, totally confused. He looked from Merry to Anneke's father and back again. He mumbled, "Germans gone? . . . The baby . . . ?" He grabbed the man by the shoulder, shook him and said, "Make sense! What are you talking about?"

"They've gone. From the whole island. They've been recalled. The Allies are pushing toward Germany. They've been recalled to defend. . . They've all gone. The Canadians have taken over!" He was beside himself. "They've set up headquarters in the house. They're setting up tents. You can come home now. There's plenty of room now. You don't have to be in this cattle barn now . . . this stable . . . "

Anneke looked up. "Stable . . . stable. . . Do you realize what that means? This is Christmas. Merry's baby was born in a stable. A miracle! At Christmas. Merry as in Merry Christmas. This is a Christmas baby. Joe and Merry, Joseph and Mary, in a stable. Animals. And there was no room at the inn. But now there is. That German soldier didn't shoot and walked away. A miracle!"

All four of them, as well as the baby got into the boat. When they arrived at the farm house. a room was prepared for the new parents. A real bed for mother and child.

Joe was ecstatic. "We have a long way to go yet before all of Holland is free, but, for now, thanks to those wonderful Canadians, the war is over for us."

THE END

All of these stories are copyright 2017 and 2018 by Arie Van der Ende. All rights reserved. No part of this work may be reproduced or transmitted in any form or by any means without the written permission of the copyright holder.

Made in the USA
Columbia, SC
25 September 2020